GLORIA'S SECRET

Damien Dsoul

Gloria's Secret
Published in 2025 by
House of Erotica
www.houseoferoticabooks.com
an imprint of
Andrews UK Limited
www.andrewsuk.com

CONTENTS

1

Gloria lay in bed flipping through a *Victoria's Secret* catalogue when her husband burst into the room, slamming the door against the wall. She had seen his car pull into the driveway from her window. She had heard his tires squealed when he braked to a stop. That told her all she needed to know—he was mad as fuck.

And it wasn't even 6:00 pm yet.

"How are you, darling?" she said to him, still not looking up from her magazine.

"You had to do it, didn't you?" her husband fumed as he approached the bed. His jacket was open. His face was all red and he was sweating and breathing hard from having raced up the stairs. "Why the fuck did you do it, Gloria? Why would you dare?"

"I've no idea what you're talking about, Lem," she replied in a cool voice.

"Don't give me that shit!" He smacked the magazine from her hand, forcing her to look at him. "You fucked him, didn't you? I know you did, so don't lie—I saw the video."

"Did you, Lem?"

"You fucked him here, in this room—*ON OUR FUCKING BED!* You screwed Morris, our fucking gardener. You kept hollering his name."

"Yes, I did," she flashed her eyes at him nonchalantly. "And I'd do it again whether you want me to or not."

Lem gasped. He felt the energy drain from him. He'd arrived home boiling with hot anger, getting ready to explode. That didn't seem to be the case anymore.

"Why did you do it, Gloria?" he pleaded. "Ain't I... haven't I done right with you?"

Gloria slid off the bed and stood facing him. "You have, darling. But there's something I want. Something every horny woman wants. Something you've never once thought to give to me. Do you want to know what that is, Lem?"

"What?"

"This."

He winced when her hand grabbed at his crotch. His penis came alive in his pants. Except it was unconvincing.

"This is what I want, Lem," Gloria declared. "What I've always wanted. Yes, I know you've got all the money in the world. I know you can spoil me many times over. But diamonds aren't always a girl's best friend. A diamond's worthless compared to a thick black cock. And you've never had the goods to give to me whenever we make love, darling."

"But... if it had to be anybody, why the fucking gardener?"

She gave a throaty laugh. "Morris has what I want, babe. He's strong. He's black, and he's got a strong cock between his legs and he knows how to use it. Unlike you. You're a wimp compared to him."

"Morris is our gardener, Gloria. *He's our fucking gardener!*"

"Yes, I know that, Lem," she snapped back. "But that's what he is to you; to me, he's what I desire in a man."

Gloria sat back on the bed and raised her skirt for him to see she was bare underneath. She spread her vulva apart with two fingers to reveal her pink moistness to him.

"Yes, we did fuck in here," she said. "We've been fucking almost a week now. I basically seduced him. He was afraid, but I told him it's OK. I even told him you'd love it. I couldn't hide it from you anymore, so I filmed us fucking and texted you that clip you watched. Come here, darling."

Lem came to the bed and sat beside her. His eyes were all over his wife, appraising her beautiful figure, wondering how any man other than himself would defile her without him knowing.

"Would you love to feel my pussy, babe?" She took his hand and brought it to her crotch. "Morris's cock is so big, I can barely take him whenever he fucks me. It's too bad you're never around to hear me scream. Come, I want you to taste me."

Gloria maneuvered backwards on the bed and gestured at Lem to come forward. He brought his face to her crotch and started eating out her pussy. She moaned and panted with delight.

He imagined Morris fucking his wife.

He pictured them rolling over the bed.

He imagined being there listening to Gloria scream…

"I told him to come over later this evening," Gloria cooed. "I want him to fuck me tonight. And I want you to be around to watch. I know you love playing with your pecker whenever you watch porn. This time you're going to see it live. Will you want that, darling."

Lem raised his face to mumble, "Ye… Yes… Yes, I'd love to."

He continued tasting his wife's pussy. He wondered if Morris had cummed inside his wife like they often did in those interracial movies he loved sneaking off to watch downstairs in his library. He couldn't wait for it to happen.

"What day is he coming over?"

"He'll be here this weekend. And also, darling, you're going to clean his cock for me!"

2

Gloria said goodbye then ended her call and turned to her husband and said, "That was Morris, darling. He's on his way. He'll be here in twenty minutes, so you have to hurry."

Lem looked confused. They were upstairs in the bedroom. It was almost 4:15 pm on a Saturday evening.

"Hurry? Hurry where?"

"Hurry and hide, silly. You can place yourself in the coat room out in the hallway downstairs. It's tight, but you can fit inside and watch from there. I'll leave the living room door open so you can watch."

"Gloria…"

"And for God's sake, don't wear any shoes," she indicated at his footwear. "Put them aside and walk in your stockings. The less noise you make the better or you might alarm him."

"Gloria…"

"How does my hair look, by the way?" she ran her fingers through her locks while admiring herself in her vanity mirror. "Do you think Morris will like it? What about my dress?" She wore a burgundy dress that had a low-cut section that showed off her cleavage. "Remember this is the one you bought me last Valentine's Day. I love the way it shows off my bust line. I can't wait for Morris to undress me. Don't you agree, darling?"

"Yeah, swell. Gloria, will you please listen for a minute?"

"What, Lem, what?" she snapped irritably then looked at her watch. "Time is running. I already told him you won't be home."

"Yes, yes, I know—you don't want me running into Morris because you haven't told him I'm aware, and he's coming right now and you want me to go hide in the coat closet and watch. I get all of that. But Gloria, won't it look stupid of me hiding in my own house? Can't you just go ahead and tell him—It's not like I'm gonna hurt me or that I'm mad. But it'd be a lot better if I'm free to watch than you sneaking me inside a closet, don't you think?"

Gloria sighed and spoke warmly. "Lem, darling, we've been over this already, remember? Morris is a shy fellow. But like I promised, after today I'm going to tell him everything. I just want you to watch this one time. Remember you've bugged me about that so many times already, right?"

Lem made a sad face and nodded sheepishly.

"I thought so. Now, are you going to be a good boy and stay quiet and watch, or do I have to lock you out?"

"No… no, you don't need to do that. I'll be good and quiet."

She smiled and gave him a kiss. "That's my darling. Now, let's hurry. It's almost time."

They went downstairs together. Lem took off his shoes before hiding himself inside the coat room. He was upset and simultaneously jumpy with excitement at what was about to unfold in his home.

Gloria went and sat in the living room and put on the TV. She picked up the remote and flipped to the Adult Channel and relaxed to enjoy a porn flick that was already playing. She looked at her watch. Morris ought to be here already, she thought with angst. She admired her pump heels as well her dress; she could not wait to get fucked.

DIINNNGGG-DOOOONNNGGG!

Gloria came off the sofa and bounded out of the living room. She was buoyant with excitement as she went and unlocked the front door.

Morris, her husband's erstwhile gardener and her lover stood there on the front steps looking handsome and laidback cool in a t-shirt and chinos pants. Gloria grabbed him by his shirt before he had a chance to say anything and propelled him into the house.

"Easy babe," he said after she slammed shut the door. "Slow down. I told you I'd be here."

Gloria hugged and kissed him like she was thirty and he was a glass of water.

"I'd wanted you to get here sooner. Come, let's go into the living room."

"One quick thing, your man ain't around, is he?"

"Lem? Hell no. I told you he's out of town and won't get home until midnight."

She pulled him along and sat him down on the sofa she previously occupied while planting herself on his lap. The porn flick was still on, showcasing a trio of black men gangbanging a pretty lass.

"This what you been watching?" Morris asked.

"I was, yes. But I'm glad you're here so I don't have to anymore. Do you like my dress?"

"Yeah, you look beautiful." He caressed her thigh. "Love your high heels, too."

"Oh, thank you, babe. You look like you did some working out today."

"Whenever I can. I tried sleeping when I got home in the afternoon, but no luck."

"Aw, that's too bad. Here, let me help you to unwind."

Gloria got up from his thighs and wet her lips with her tongue as she unzipped his fly.

Out in the hallway, the coat door inched open enough for Lem to spy what was going on beyond the living room doorway. He could not at first make out Morris's face, but observed Gloria drop to her knees between his legs. He stretched further into view and saw she was sucking her lover's cock. Lem grew rock hard as he watched. This was what he had pleaded for days for Gloria to allow him to watch them in action. His dream had finally come through and he loved it.

Gloria went on blowing Morris's pipe with gusto. She rummaged inside his pants to grab at his nuts and sucked on those too. Morris responded positively as she expected. He pressed her head downward to ingest more of his prick.

Her mouth let go of his cock with a 'plop' sound as she then rose to her feet. Morris kicked off his shoes and unbuckled his belt and shoved his pants down his thighs. Gloria fell down into his arms. Morris lifted her dress and saw she was bare underneath. She straddled him and slipped his cock between her legs. Her pussy resisted at first but with a little lubrication he gained further inside to stretch her cunt.

"Uuuhhhhh, yes, babe," she whimpered as she settled her butt on his thigh, feeling his cock get massive in her pussy. "Ahhhh God, I've missed you, babe. I fucking missed your cock!"

Morris squeezed her ass as she took more of his cock.

Gloria moaned and wrapped both arms around his shoulders.

Lem stared wide-eyed at his wife's buttock riding her lover.

Gloria moaned as she rocked her hips and bounced her butt on her lover's thick rod. They locked lips and she murmured inarticulate words of pleasure to him. She flung her head backwards and caught brief sighting of her husband jerking his penis while watching and filming them from beyond the doorway with his cell phone. She went on bucking her hips; her groans went in sync with Morris matching her rhythm.

She alighted from Morris and he came to his feet and peeled off his t-shirt then got her bend forward on the sofa. Gloria gripped the sofa's fabric and squealed when Morris thrust into her harder this time. He grabbed her waist and fed her long strokes of his cock at first, rubbing his palm over her butt, then got to fucking her faster.

Lem watched everything. He watched Morris's buttock muscles tense each time he rammed into Gloria. He listened to her undulating cries with gusto. He could not believe this was what his wife had been enjoying all this while with him being too clueless to know. He continued watching. Afterwards he looked downward and realized he had unconsciously ejaculated in his pants.

He looked up and saw Morris was fucking Gloria harder; the sound of their bodies slamming each other and the cries she gave were almost intertwined. It did not take long for Morris to climax inside Gloria.

Lem hurried back into the coat closet and quietly shut the door. Inside, he unbuttoned his pants and scooped as much of his semen in his palm and licked it off. It tasted good. But he knew the ultimate prize would involve tasting Morris's cum out of his wife.

3

The time was 9:26 p.m. Lem and his wife were in bed but they were far from retiring for the night.

Gloria sat upright against her pillows with her knees drawn up, moaning from the pleasure she got from Lem who lay forward on the bed with his head pressed down on her pelvis and his hands wrapped around her thighs. His lips made smacking noise as he ate every inch of her pussy.

Gloria caressed his head.

She breathed and sucked air through her lips.

She purred at him not to stop.

Lem did not intend to quit, not until he made her climax, which inevitably she did. Gloria whimpered and her hips jerked into uncontrollable spasms as she pussy squirted copiously on her husband's face. Lem took everything she had to offer and more.

He went into the bathroom to wash himself up. He as well masturbated to his satisfaction into the toilet bowl then flushed. This now was the limit of enjoyable sex he got from Gloria since finding out about her cheating habit with their black gardener.

Lem washed his hands when he was done before returning to the bedroom. Gloria had tucked her feet back into the covers and was lying down.

"That was fun," Lem said as he slid under the covers beside her.

"It truly was," she agreed. "I checked while you were in there. You did a thorough clean-up this time. Thanks."

"My pleasure, darling."

Morris had for the past week been steadfast with regards to bedding Gloria whenever he came by to perform his chores on their garden. He had left their home an hour ago having fucked Gloria downstairs in the living room while Lem once again had stayed hidden in the coat closet, jerking off while watching them fuck; he had even filmed them together with his phone. Their affair was now in its third week and Morris remained unaware of Lem. Gloria stubbornly hadn't yet revealed the truth to him, regardless of Lem's pleas. Lem was equally frustrated with whatever reason she had for keeping both men from finding out about each other to whichever ends he couldn't fathom.

"For God's sake, enough for this high-falluting suspense," Lem pleaded amidst his grumble. "Why can't you quit playing and tell him about me? I promised already I'll continue to be your slave no matter what. Why the delay?"

"Patience, darling," she said soothingly. "There's a new turn of events I haven't told you about yet."

"What is it now? What new event are you cooking up?"

She turned to face him. "It's like this. Morris likes me a lot, the same way I do of him. But since we started, I've got this crazy idea that it won't feel right keeping him all to myself. I feel the need to share him with someone else. With someone who's just as nasty and dirty a slut as I am."

"Sounds intriguing. Who have you got in mind? I don't know any of our rich friends whose wife fucks around."

"That's because you've never paid attention about this lifestyle before I showed it to you, sweetheart. There's plenty of white women out there who're doing this; even some of your friends. But there's especially one who's just as much a fuck-slut as I am. She's close to you, but I'll bet you're clueless about her. Care to take a guess?"

Lem thought for a moment, then shook his head. "You're right, honey. I can't think of any. Who is it, the Mulberrys living down the street?"

"No, not Rachel," she laughed. "I'm talking about Zia. Your cousin."

Lem looked at her, thinking Gloria had cracked a silly joke. When he realized she wasn't, his eyes flew open as well his mouth slacken in stunned surprise.

"Nooooo… not Zia?" he croaked.

"Yes, that Zia," Gloria emphasized.

"Come on, stop joking here. Zia doesn't screw around like a tramp. There's no way that's ever possible. Her husband's a Deacon for Christ's sake!"

"I'm sorry to disappoint you, darling," Gloria chuckled, deriving pleasure from having crushed her husband's spirit with decisive ease. "Whatever you thought you knew about your sweet cousin is all wrong. Zia's fucked more cocks than I can count; I know this because I've played with her before."

Lem looked at her with incredulous pair of eyes. "For real, Gloria?"

"Yes, for real, Lem. I've told her already about Morris. She said she can't wait to meet him."

Gloria switched off her lamp light. Lem did the same to his, plunging the bedroom in darkness as they lay beside each other.

"Oh God, not Zia," Lem groaned. "I can't believe this."

"Don't worry, darling. It'll be fun. Who knows, she probably won't mind you eating her pussy too," she chuckled as she lay her face against his chest. "Good night, sweetheart."

"Goodnight," Lem muttered.

Gloria was asleep in an instant. For Lem, he remained awake picturing his cousin out there, hitting bars and night spots, looking for viable men to spend the night with. He pictured the men fucking her in motel rooms and outdoors in the back seat of their cars. To think that like Gloria she too brought men to her home to fuck was scary to imagine. It was agony for Lem conjuring up such images.

But as his breathing deepened and he slipped gradually into that void known as deep sleep, an impressive imagery began playing actively before his eyes. This one involved Morris taking turns fucking Gloria then his cousin. He pictured Morris fucking Zia from behind while Gloria lay beside them on the bed fingering her cunt. The moment came when Morris ejaculated inside Zia while she held onto him as he did. After watching Morris pull out of her, Lem imagined himself suddenly jump out of his hiding place and rush over to gobble the thick semen oozing out of his sister's cunt.

Lem was smiling to himself as he conjured up this indelible part in his head. His penis grew hard then eventually limp as he fell asleep.

4

It was a blustery Saturday afternoon when Lem said goodbye to his friend and neighbor Eric Mulberry at the country club where they often hung out and played tennis. They had spared with each other for two straight sets. Lem enjoyed the sweat. Afterwards they broke for lunch and talked neighborhood gossip before Lem decided calling it a day.

He drove leisurely back home. Gloria's car was parked in the driveway as well another vehicle—a grey Mercedes. Lem knew who it belonged to and it made him suddenly queasy knowing who was waiting for him inside. He came out of his car carrying his tennis racket and gym bag and went into his ultra-modern home.

Lem caught the sound of laughter coming from the living room. It stopped when he shut the door. Gloria, his wife, came to greet him.

"How was your game, darling?" she kissed him, then relieved him of the items he carried.

"It was great. I spent time with Eric; he sends his love. Where's Zia?"

"She's been waiting to see you," she took his hand and led him towards the living room. "We both have been," she added.

Lem's cousin Zia sat on the sofa smoking a cigarette and watching a movie. Everything about her was bold and audacious; that included her feminine aura. Gloria left them with each other and took Lem's racket and gym bag upstairs. Lem looked at the TV as he sat down beside her and gasped when he saw it was a porn flick—two black men took turns fucking a gorgeous brunette. The woman looked familiar. It took less than a minute to realize it was actually his cousin Zia.

"What the fuck is this?" he asked awestruck.

"What do you think it is, Lem?" she replied smarmily. "It's an outtake of a porn shoot I made with two studs last week that I wanted Gloria to see."

"Christ almighty."   .

"Oh, stop being a downer, Lem. Doesn't it make you hard? Don't worry, I'll send you a copy once the actual movie gets out."

"For God's sake, Zia. This is insane."

Zia laughed. "Quit your silly pretense game, Lem. Gloria's kept me abreast of everything, including the way you love to eat her out. Black cock is always the best, especially their cum."

"How long have you been doing this, Zia? Was it before you married Jeff?"

"Way back in high school, and yes, it was way before Jeff and I met." She smoked her cigarette. "I'm sorry you had to find out the way you did, but this is who I am."

"You're so proud of yourself cheating on Jeff this whole time, aren't you?"

"I don't cheat on Jeff," she declared. "Why do I need to when he knows everything. And he's very OK with it. Really, you shouldn't be all too surprised now that Gloria's indoctrinated you into it. It's in our genes, Lem."

"What's in our genes?"

"Fucking black men, Lem. Getting fucked by them, worshipping them… that's what we were made for. It took you this long to figure that out."

Gloria sauntered into the room cradling her phone. "You've got forty minutes to shower and change, dear. I just got off talking to Morris—he's on his way."

Lem stared at Gloria, baffled. "What do you mean?"

"Morris, darling," Gloria snapped impatiently. "I told you last time he's coming to spend time with Zia and I. You can stay and watch if you want, or you can leave. Whichever choice you want."

"Do stay and watch, Lem," Zia teased. "I'd love for you to stay and watch. Gloria tells me his cock is amazing and he knows how to use it."

"Quit it, Zia," Lem groaned.

"There's gonna be plenty of creampie for you, sissy," she continued.

"I'd better head upstairs then and wash up," he said to Gloria before leaving the room.

Lem trampled up the stairs, grunting as he worked to get out of his clothes. He stumbled clumsily as he shoved open the bedroom door and kicked off my shoes. He stumbled into the bathroom and hurried with washing away his sweat. Finished in record time, he scrambled for something decent to wear, not even bothering to dry myself. Thirty-six minutes had passed by the time Lem trundled down the stairs, gasping with his cell phone in hand. He almost expected to find Morris in his living room already when he got there but was disappointed when it was just wife and his cousin sipping wine.

Gloria and Zia.

Two gorgeous women waiting for a lone black man.

Even he felt the anticipation in the room.

Gloria turned to him and said, "Well? Shouldn't you be hiding in the closet right now?"

"Do we really have to go through this again?" Lem whined, knowing already it was pointless to argue.

"Lem Jessup Carter, don't make me have to burst a nerve on you right now," she snapped. "Morris will be here any second."

She stopped when the doorbell sounded and everyone stopped for a moment. Gloria glared at Lem; it was the signal for him to up and disappear. He scrambled to the coatroom door and slipped inside just as Gloria went to answer the front door; Zia appraised herself then resumed watching her movie.

Gloria soon returned and this time she was not alone. An athletic black man with a bashful smile walked alongside her. Gloria introduced Morris to Zia; it was plain obvious why he was there. Lem peeped from inside the coatroom. His penis stood erect in his shorts. He breathed through his mouth as he watched.

Morris sat on the sofa between the women, both of whom pressed against him. Zia cooed as she caressed his arms while Gloria crossed her leg over his thigh. They wasted no time having their own fun.

Zia and Gloria pretty much fought over Morris. He went back and forth kissing either while they rubbed their feet against his thigh. Gloria raised her top and offered her lover her breasts to play with.

Zia slipped a hand under his t-shirt.

She marveled at his chiseled abs.

Strong, black and hard—just like her men.

Morris turned his attention to her and Zia propped open her blouse for him to squeeze her tits into his mouth. Gloria did the honor of unbuckling his belt then unzipping his fly. His cock was hard and waiting. Gloria glanced towards the closet where she knew her husband was hiding and watching. She glanced in his direction as she then introduced her lover's cock into her mouth.

Lem had a good view of Gloria blowing her lover. Myriad of extreme emotions danced in his head. Anger... Jealousy... Envy... Desire... and unnerving anticipation of the impending sex bout. Pre-cum stained the inside of his shorts as he grabbed onto his cock for dear life. He was gasping harder just as sweat popped steadily on his brow.

Is it getting hot in here, he asked himself, *or is it just me?*

Zia, not wanting to be left out, slid down the sofa to join Gloria in tasting her lover's erection. They cradled Morris's prick between them like it was King Arthur's sword. They purred as they swore allegiance kissing each end of his Excalibur, sucking his shaft, swallowing his nutssack. Morris caressed their hair, guiding them to where he wanted them.

From inside the coatroom, Lem held up his phone to record the event as Morris extracted his feet out of his jeans then came to his feet. Gloria and Zia too stripped out of their outfits and discarded them on the floor. They assumed the doggy position on the sofa.

"Make a choice, babe," Gloria cooed as she twerked her booty at him. "Which pussy would you want to go in first?"

Morris stroked his cock while admiring both women's buttock, smiling as he thought to himself which pussy he wanted to fuck first.

Even Lem, too, wanted to know. "Please take Zia," he muttered under his breath.

His mind made up, Morris advanced toward the women.

5

Morris took aim at Zia's pussy slit.

Lem peeped through a hole in the coatroom's door and for a moment held his breath as he watched.

"Give it to her, Morris," Lem's wife Gloria jeered as she spread Zia's ass cheeks apart for him. "Go on, give it to her. She wants that cock of yours."

Morris's cock punctured Zia's pussy walls. Her body jerked and shook in response. Morris stopped for a moment as her body broke into a shiver and she exhaled a lengthy moan. Her pussy gave off an exquisite fart. He waited for her to get acclimatized to his girth then slowly slipped further into her moist cunt. Zia grabbed at the sofa's headrest. Her face curled into a mask of pleasure and pain. This is exactly what she had sought when Gloria invited her over.

Gloria fingered Zia's anus while taking in the sight of her lover's cock sliding all the way into her pussy. She couldn't help herself glancing toward the coatroom, picturing her husband encumbered inside, jerking off his pecker to the sight of what was being done to his cousin. Little did he know she had another surprise to spring on him.

But first…

Morris sucked air through his gritted teeth and shook his head side to side as he went on fucking Zia. He, too, was enjoying the feel of her tight pussy around his shaft. Such a wonderful feeling unlike anything a man can ever afford to enjoy. The fact that he now had two pussies to fuck made things very pleasant to imagine. He only hopped he didn't blow it by ejaculating too soon.

Gloria leaned towards him and they shared a lengthy kiss. "I told you I was going to have a surprise for you when you come by," she said.

"Yeah, you weren't lying, babe," he replied.

"How good does her pussy feel, babe?"

"*Uhhh* terrific," he gasped. "So tight and good."

"Well, you'd better save some strength for me."

Gloria assumed similar position on the sofa as Zia did beside her; she reached downward and moaned as she rubbed at her clit. Morris looked at her and knew that was the signal that she demanded her turn of his cock.

Lem was gasping and sweating profusely inside the coatroom. His hand was busy jerking his cock hard. Already he had sprayed semen all over his shorts and licked it off his fingers and still he remained hard. He had never been as excited ever before as he was now. Not after watching his dirty whore of a cousin getting fucked by another man. He pictured himself mentioning this to her husband Jeff and tried to imagine what his response would be. He recalled Zia saying he was aware of her sexual peccadilloes, so it would not be of any harm to him hearing more about her actions.

He focused his attention to the sight of Morris as he was now switching places and fucking Gloria. Oh, how bad Lem couldn't wait for him to bust his nut inside Gloria up so he could spend the rest of the afternoon soaking his cum down her throat when she got a chance to sit on his face. *But what if Morris opted saving his semen for Zia instead?* Well, never one to be condemned for committing incest, he would have to figure out some other means of having a taste, won't he?

Morris balanced his weight upon the sofa, hunched over Gloria and was thrusting deeper into her cunt. From Lem's point of view, he saw his nuts-sac slap repeatedly against his wife ass while he rammed his cock inside her. Gloria was groaning her head off like she did not have a care in the world who heard her screams.

"Ohh yes! Yes... fuck that pussy, darling!" she gasped over and over.

Zia came and knelt behind them, nearly blocking Lem's view of the action, as she got to rimming Lem's ass and slid downward to Gloria's. Lem was jerking and gasping harder. He accidently bumped his knuckles against the coatroom's door and had to catch himself. His excitement was bearing toward being noticed. Gloria would definitely get upset if he made himself too obvious. All the time he pleaded with her about making him known to her lover and here he was still suffering for lack of it.

He ejaculated in his hand a second time. Lem cursed under his breath and was licking semen off his fingers as he had done before when he heard what sounded like Gloria's voice loud and clear, almost as if she was standing close by.

"I'm sorry, Morris darling, but there's someone I want you so much to meet," said Gloria.

Lem felt his heart leap into his throat when he heard her say that. He did not want to believe what he thought he had just heard. He peeped out the hole and too late saw Gloria approach the closet door. He felt his penis shrink into his gut when he heard the lock turn seconds before the coatroom's door flung open to reveal him to the occupants of the living room.

Gloria stood there smiling at Lem. Behind her, Lem saw Morris standing beside the sofa with Zia attending to his cock with a look of surprise in his face as he suddenly realized they had been watched the entire time.

"Come on out, honey," Gloria gestured at Lem. "It's time I introduce you to Morris."

* * *

Lem stood there in the coatroom embarrassed by the moment. He realized belatedly that he had his thumb stuck in his mouth still licking off his semen while staring dumbfounded at Gloria. Lem carefully stepped out of the coatroom like he could not believe he was actually there. He tried not to glance past his wife at the sight of his cousin while Morris looked at him stunned.

"The fuck are you doing, Gloria?" he whispered to her as she took his hand and led him into the living room. Lem hurriedly tucked his penis back into his shorts with his face glowing red with embarrassment.

"No need to be bashful, honey," said Gloria. "We're all adults here. You've always wanted to meet the man who's been fucking me all this time. Well, here he is, our gardener." She turned to Morris. "Morris, you do know my husband, don't you? I'm sorry but he's known about us since. I've waited for the perfect moment to introduce you both and today absolutely felt like it."

Neither Morris nor Lem knew what response to give each other. They tried not to make eye contact at first until Gloria tapped their arms, snapping them to reality.

Husband and gardener.

Cuck and lover.

What were the odds they would haplessly meet like this?

"Are you boys gonna shake hands or what?" Zia asked.

"I think they have already," Gloria answered before turning to her husband. "You wanted to meet Morris face to face, well, now you have. If you don't mind, I'm going to enjoy more of his cock now. You can sit down and watch and maybe get yourself a nice bonus when I'm done, or you can return to the closet where you were. I really don't care."

Lem wanted to say something in his defense. Too late, Gloria turned to her lover, grabbed him by his cock and pulled him away from Zia. She rested on the sofa and flung her legs apart. Morris glanced at Lem as he then came at Gloria who caught the glance he gave Lem.

"Don't mind him, dear," she said. "He loves to watch. He's been watching us fuck since we started. Pretend he's not here and drive that cock inside me. I'm so fucking wet."

Morris rubbed his penis against her vulva before thrusting all the way inside her cunt.

"Awwhhhhh yeah!" Gloria cried. Her body broke into spasms as he reclined on top of her, resting his arms against her shoulders and spreading his legs apart to get a better traction.

"Awww... Aaahhhh give it to me, Morris," she grabbed his shoulders, urging him to fuck her harder. "Go ahead, fuck me. Don't stop... *make my husband jealous!*"

Morris fucked Gloria harder, just the way she wanted. Zia sat beside them massaging her pussy and playing with her nipples while she waited for her turn. Morris pulled out of Gloria and went and fed her pussy with his meat. He hammered Zia well enough until returning back to fucking Gloria. Neither of them paid any attention to Lem. He had resumed jerking his cock while waiting for the inevitable moment he knew was coming. He could almost taste it. Even from listening to his wife's cries he knew her lover was abound to ejaculate any second.

The moment happened and Morris groaned and muttered expletives as he pressed his torso against Gloria. His hips jerked spasmodically as he emptied his nuts-sac inside her. Gloria, too, held him down and locked her ankles against his thighs.

"Ohhhh fuck… yes, babe! Yes… yes, darling… gimme all your seed! I want it all!"

Morris remained on top Gloria for more than a minute, gasping as he unleashed everything. Eventually he pulled out of her and her pussy spurted a bubble of thick semen.

Lem sprang into action and dashed towards his wife.

6

Lem thought of nothing as he dashed toward Gloria and started eating out her pussy. He thought nothing of Morris, who stood beside them watching, having just concluded fucking his wife, or of his cousin Zia, who too, was there to see everything for herself. None of this registered in his mind besides wanting so bad to taste Morris's cum out of his wife's pussy. It was something he had waited this long to enjoy.

He held Gloria's legs apart then buried his face upon her twat. He attacked with his lips like a rabbit burrowing into the earth; like a dog digging for a hidden bone, except in this case it was the ounce of thick semen percolating inside her pussy. Lem overheard a crackle of laughter. It sounded like it was coming from Zia.

His wife pressed his head down her crotch.

She jerked her pelvis upward at his face.

His tongue slid and probed her cunt for morsels of cum.

"That's a good boy," Gloria cooed while still caressing her husband's head, simultaneously moaning from the exquisite kisses he gave to her pussy. "Yeah, clean up my pussy, babe. Uuhhh yes… yes, that's it. Alright, honey. Come, there's more I want you to do."

Lem pulled away for a moment to breathe in some air. The lower part of his face appeared wet and sticky. He ran his hand across his lips and it came away with his wife's cum juice, and proceeded to lick it clean. His eyes burned with yearning hunger the likes he had never experienced before. He was so willing at that moment to do anything to please his wife; he so much wanted to go the distance for her.

"Hold on, darling," Gloria stopped him before he could walk away. "There's somebody else in this room that needs your attention." She turned to Morris who was busy kissing Zia. His cock remained semi-erect and hung like a pendulum down his crotch.

"I want you to clean his cock for me," Gloria instructed her husband. "Would you do that for me, darling? I know you want to. We've talked about it before, remember?"

Indeed they had, and more than once… but even then he never thought she was serious until now. It was too late to decline her wish.

"Morris darling, please come over. My husband wants to properly welcome you into our home. Just let him do this one thing for you." She grasped his cock and stroked his hard-on then turned to Lem. "Be a good boy and clean his cock for me."

"Yeah, go ahead, Lem," Zia cheered. She was leaning over the couch, not wanting to miss a moment of what was about to happen.

Lem inched forward with his mouth open.

Gloria drew Morris's cock closer towards his mouth.

Lem locked his lips around Morris's cock and started sucking him.

Zia clapped ecstatically. Gloria was all smiles watching her husband gulp her lover's penis. She sat back and played with herself while Lem went on sucking him.

"Keep sucking that black cock, darling," she murmured. "Suck it like you love eating my pussy. I'll bet you can't wait for him to fuck me again, can you?"

Lem murmured an affirmation as he continued choking on the black cock that now filled his mouth. He sputtered gobs of saliva off the side of his lips. It was genuine punishment and he could feel a throbbing ache in his jaw muscles as he continued blowing Morris's girth. Eventually he stopped and bowed his head as he began to retch and cough. He gagged a couple of times, hoicking and swallowing back his spit. Strings of saliva dribbled from his mouth and landed on the carpet.

"You did good, darling," said Gloria after he had reclaimed himself. "Don't worry. With time, I know you'll get better at doing that."

Zia thought it was her turn now and locked her arm around Morris. "About time I got to enjoy a bit of you before I leave. Where's your bedroom at, Gloria?"

"I know where it's at," Morris said. "Let's go."

Lem crumbled on the sofa beside Gloria. They watched Morris and Zia leave the room in each other's arms while they remained as they were. The movie that was earlier playing on the TV had long stopped.

Gloria tapped Lem's arm. "We'd better go see what they're up to."

Lem helped her to her feet and stopped to wipe his palm on his shorts. Gloria picked up her clothes including those of Zia and laid them on the sofa before they then went up the stairs to their bedroom. Zia's moaning voice was echoing inside the room before they even opened the door.

They opened the bedroom door and peeped inside.

Zia was on her elbows and knees on top of the bed. Her back was angled downward with her ass sticking upward while Morris balanced himself in a crouching stance and was fucking her with full might. There was the sound of loud clapping each time he slammed against her buttock. The thunderclap was then followed by Zia's whimpering moans. She gripped the bed sheets and her body jerked forward with each pounding Morris gave her. His backside glistened with sweat; he held on to Zia's hips hard and tight, grunting with exertion with each pounding he rammed upon her.

"Aww, they look so good together, don't you think?" Gloria said to Lem. "Morris finally gets to christen our bedroom, honey."

"What are you talking about? You said before that you and him have fucked in here."

"I know, darling. But then you weren't around to watch now were you?"

Morris gave one final thrust that knocked Zia to fall flat on her face and pulled out of her. Lem focused his eyes on his massive cock. He saw it was spilling cum onto the sheets. He could not help but lick his lips at the thought of having another go at getting to worship his cock once more. Zia had already seen him do it downstairs so there was absolutely nothing to be ashamed of anymore.

Gloria left him standing by the doorway to go to the bed to join her lover. Zia made room for her on the bed as she laid on her back and spread her legs and gestured at Morris to come have another go at her. Morris swiped a stream of sweat off his brow then went and plugged her pussy.

"Get over here, Lem," Zia called out.

Lem went to her. Zia indicated at him to get on the floor which he did.

"Lie on your back for me," she demanded.

Lem did as ordered. He spied Morris on his king-sized bed fucking Gloria, listening to Gloria gasp and plea for him to fuck her harder. The sound of their bodies clashing was enough to tell him Morris was doing exactly that.

Zia came and stood over Lem's face and then lowered herself to a crotch over him. Lem raised his head, wondering if he was going to perform the same clean-up exercise on his cousin as he had done his wife, but gasped in momentous surprise when Zia instead squirted down on him. She crackled uproariously while she did.

"There," she murmured when she was done. "That feels good. Now you're a sissy," she added.

7

It was late in the evening when Lem came out of the house, got into his car and pulled out of his driveway. He had changed into a different set of clothes having showered once more. His cousin Zia had already left for home although somewhat reluctant about it. She claimed it had been almost a week since she had gotten well fucked by a stud like Gloria's man.

Lem drove to a McDonalds restaurant not far from home and drove back twenty-five minutes later laden with take-away snacks he had bought. He entered his house and headed for the kitchen. There he took the snacks out of their separate bags and laid them on plates which then went on a tray, including sodas he had brought and carried them up the stairs to the bedroom.

He knocked on the door before entering.

Gloria lay in bed alone; there was no Morris there beside her. Lem looked around and didn't see any sight of his clothes anywhere.

"He had to leave suddenly," Gloria said. "But he said he'll be back later."

"It wasn't because of me, was it?"

Lem came and laid the tray on the bed. The sheets tumbled off Gloria's body when she sat up to inspect what he had brought her.

"Of course it wasn't because of you. You should stop thinking so negative." She took a bite off her cheeseburger he had bought. "Morris doesn't carry any guilt towards you," she added.

"Well, you and him do look good together. What did Zia think about him?"

"What do you think? You watched them fuck, didn't you? She fucking loved it."

"He's got a big cock," Lem remarked. "When you got me to suck him, I could barely contain him in my mouth."

"You loved it, didn't you?"

Lem shrugged at first, but then blushed. "Sort of."

"Not sort of, darling. I knew you loved it." Gloria chowed the rest of her cheeseburger before then attacking her fries. "There's something else I haven't yet told you. Morris needed money, so I gave him one of your credit cards."

"What?"

"You're going to have to increase whatever it is you're paying him, because it's peanuts, darling. I won't want my lover wearing cheap-ass clothes whenever he comes around."

Lem looked at Gloria stunned by her words.

"You actually gave him one of my credit cards? Couldn't you have bothered asking me first?"

"I could, but I was worried you might say no. Let's face it, you'd either say no, or you'd bitch and groan about it all day, and I didn't want to hear none of that."

Lem's feature turned sullen. "Still you should have told me…"

"You're right, I should have, and I'm sorry I didn't," she said it so fast it sounded dismissive. "But I've already done it. Besides, you've got plenty of credit cards. Missing out on one won't hurt."

Gloria went on eating her snack meal while Lem looked like he wanted to fall sick.

* * *

Another week went by before they got to see Morris. It was a Saturday when he showed up in a polo shirt and khaki shorts that he had purchased thanks to Lem's credit card. He brought with him a bag that contained his garden tools.

It so happened on that day Lem was throwing a get-together party at his backyard when Morris arrived. Some of his neighbors were there, including Eric and Rachel Mulberry. Gloria was enjoying the swimming pool along with other friends of hers; Lem wore an apron and was

As it turned out, Gloria was wrong. One of her friend was wondering whatever was taking her long to return with a fresh bottle of champagne.

Rachel excused herself from the others and ventured into the house to check on whatever was keeping Gloria. She didn't find her in the kitchen and her eyes happened on Gloria's empty glass where she had left it. Rachel went further into the house and up the stairs. She got to the main bedroom door and was about knocking when she thought she heard what sounded like explicit groans coming from inside. She tried the door handle but found it locked. She placed her ear to the door instead and it dawned on her what she was listening to.

* * *

Gloria laid on her back on the bed with her feet hanging in the air, courtesy of Morris holding her ankles apart. He was all serious business as he fed his dick into her cunt. Gloria's body jerked in response, followed by a soulful groan that seeped through her lips. Her hands ran over her body, stopping to squeeze her breasts and pinch her nipples while exhaling from the overwhelming vigor of his girth.

Her panties with her bra lay discarded on the floor. Gloria kept levitating her pelvis to keep up with his repeated slamming. She tapped his hips, urging him to up his pace and give it to her hard. Morris already had sweat popping on his brow. His shaft pulled out of her pussy lips laden with her cum. He dug both hands under her backside and lifted her off the bed. Gloria locked her legs behind his back while he cradled her buttock in his hands and they grunted near simultaneously in each other's face as he shoved her back and forth on his cock. Gloria twirled her head from the abrupt motion. Morris locked lips with her and she groaned even louder as he fucked her with the perfect rhythm she wanted.

She felt his cock getting bigger in her cunt, and from his strenuous breathing knew he intended climaxing any moment. Gloria came down from him and fell to her knees and finished him off by sucking his cock hard and loud.

Morris gasped.

His chest heaved.

His mouth hung open and he groaned as he let himself go inside her mouth.

* * *

Minutes later Gloria was back in her swimsuit outfit as she then unlocked the bedroom door. She blew a kiss at her lover and promised to be back for him later before leaving the room. She waltzed back down the stairs and ran into Lem in the kitchen. They shared a distinct glanced that spoke more than words.

"Morris is still upstairs," she came and whispered into his ear. "Go up and look after him for me, darling."

She kissed his cheek then fetched a wine bottle out of the fridge and a clean glass then went out to join her friends by the pool. Rachel was back there waiting for her. She gave no indication of what she had overheard; that would be for later.

Lem looked at his wife laughing once more with her friends. He felt the calling to go upstairs and see about her lover, and that was what he did. Unknown to him, just like with Gloria, he too would be observed by someone else.

8

There came the sound of a toilet flushing, followed by a fart noise, and then then a loud belch. The toilet door opened into an alcove beside the coatroom to reveal Rachel's husband Eric who then stepped out while still adjusting his shirt into his pants. He checked his pants to make sure he had not any noticeable stain on them, then hearing footsteps turned his head in time to see his friend Lem hurrying up the stairs like something serious was afoot.

Curiosity got the better of Eric and he decided to go upstairs to see whatever might be amiss.

He got to the top of the stairs and looked down the hallway that led to Lew's bedroom. He was familiar with the layout of his friend's home as he had been in it countless times. The bedroom door at the end of the hallway stood ajar. Eric went toward it.

He almost knocked when he came to the door but stopped himself when he heard distinct noise from within. He recognized Lew's voice when he spoke.

"May I play with it, sir?"

Then came the weird, distinct sounds—slurping, smooching type sounds that raised the hairs at the back of Eric's neck to stand attention. He recognized those sounds, as any man should. The sounds combined conjured up erotic images in the forefront of his mind. Eric looked back at the end of the hallway towards the stairs from whence he had come. He wondered for a moment whether he should desist from this place. He pressed his back against the wall while his ears absorbed the music coming from inside the room. His initial thought was that Lew was having an affair and was crazy enough to invite her over to his home. That thought was discarded from his mind when he heard a man's voice instead.

"Yeah, suck that cock."

Eric's eyes lit with horror. He edged closer to the door and managed to peep inside without being seen. What he saw was so unnerving he could not take his eyes away.

His friend Lem was kneeling before the spread legs of another man whose face Eric could not make out on account that he lay in his back on the bed. All he could see was the back of Lem's head bobbing down the man's crotch. Eric watched wide-eyed for nearly a minute before slipping away. He tip-toed back to the stairs and went outside to join their other neighbors and friends.

* * *

Morris laid on his back while his arms flung wide, caressing the sheets while soaked in the sweet ecstasy of Lem massaging his cock with his mouth and hands. He was not bisexual—at least he never considered himself one—though it was not the first time he had granted a man access to suck his cock. He considered it a novelty type of experience for himself. As Lem went on sucking his cock, he recalled the recent tryst he had enjoyed with the man's wife. That got blood pumping into his muscle and it was not long before he climaxed with satisfaction.

Lem captured his load of semen and even licked the spilled drops off Morris's thigh when he finished. He went into the bathroom to wash his face. He wiped himself dry with a towel, inspected himself in a mirror before returning to the bedroom. Morris went and stood by the window peering at the crowd outside.

"How long is the party to last?"

"It should be over in another hour. You don't plan on staying over?"

"I will. I don't have much doing back home today."

"That's great. Gloria will like that. You must be hungry. Let me go downstairs and get you something to eat."

Morris said nothing as Lem left the room.

* * *

That night while Morris fucked Gloria and Lem occupied one of several spare bedrooms in the house, down the street from them, the Mulberrys sat up in bed discussing what they had witnessed in their friend's home. They faced each other and conversed in such excited mode the likes that they had never had in a long time, not since they got married. Eric listened to his wife as she described in detail what she had heard when she rested her ear against their friends' bedroom door, then she listened as Eric talked about what he had spied inside. They unequivocally reached the same conclusion: their friends were into some kinky type of sex the likes they had never known before.

"When you were looking, did you by chance recognize the man's face?" asked Rachel, to which Eric shook his head.

"All I know is he's a black man. He laid on the bed so I couldn't make him out."

"There wasn't anyone like that at the party. I would have noticed if they were."

"No, I didn't see anyone either. He was probably in their home the entire time."

"I almost wanted to ask Gloria about it, but the other girls were around. I didn't want them knowing."

"Maybe you can if you go by tomorrow and ask," Eric suggested.

"You don't think that would be invasive?"

"You're going as a friend not someone stating a point."

"Yeah, I guess I could. But what do you think, darling? You think this whole time Lem is gay and Gloria doesn't know?"

"With what I saw today, I don't honestly know what to think. If she's unaware about him being gay, then he's done a great job this whole time of hiding it. But looking at them, you never would have known."

They shared a kiss then said good night to each other after tucking themselves into bed and switching off their bedside lamps. Their minds individually revolved around what they had witnessed that evening. Rachel imagined the crazy wild sex ongoing her in friend's bedroom the time she listened in and wished she had somehow gotten a glimpse of it. Whereas Eric replayed the image of his friend on his knees sucking another man's cock. He wished he had by some chance gotten a glimpse at Lem's face while he did it. Boy, would have been a terrific sight to see.

9

Rachel kept her word and was at her friend's door the following morning. She took with her an old DVD she had borrowed from Gloria weeks before as an excuse for her early visit. She pressed the door bell and waited.

The door opened to reveal Gloria standing in her robe.

"I hope I didn't come at a bad time," Rachel said after they had exchanged greetings and Gloria invited her inside.

"No, not really," Gloria said after accepting the DVD from her. "I was about to head upstairs and take a shower though. Would you mind waiting in the living room?"

"Sure."

Gloria dropped the DVD case on the table then Rachel by herself and hurried upstairs.

Rachel walked about the room, looking everywhere as if expecting to notice something or anything that appeared out of place or incongruous with the surrounding.

She approached the French windows that looked out into the backyard. There was a green tarp over the swimming pool, she observed. Lem's barbeque machine stood to itself beside the porch. Rachel looked past that at her friend's garden and saw two men standing there. She recognized Lem as he was bent over trimming the rose bushes. The other was a black man, tall and athletic, and he seemed to be indicating at Lem where to do his trimming. Rachel thought she had seen him around more than once before. Yes, he was the gardener. There was something odd about the two of them but could not put a finger to it. She was still staring at them when Gloria came and joined her, handing her a glass filled with wine.

"What's Lem doing?"

"He's trimming the rose flowers," Gloria responded. "What does it look like?"

"No, I'm sorry, but... isn't that your gardener?"

"He was," Gloria said, taking a sip of wine from her own glass. "Not anymore. Taking care of the garden is going to be part of Lem's job from now on. Morris is simply supervising him."

"Supervising?"

"Showing him the ropes," Gloria explained with a warm smile. "Lem has a lot to learn, and as long as Morris is around, he's going to show him how."

"There's something I should tell you," Rachel spoke with hesitation. "Yesterday I came by your door. I thought I heard... some noise coming from inside. You were inside, but I assume you weren't alone."

Gloria looked at her friend and caught meaning in her eyes. She suddenly burst into laughter; this got Rachel blushing.

"Oh, so you did listen in on me," Gloria said. "You're such an eavesdropper, Rachel."

"I'm sorry."

"Aw, don't be. But yes, I was fucking Morris yesterday when I left you and the others by the pool. Matter of fact, Morris and I have been screwing for weeks now."

"Excuse me?"

"Screwing, as in we're fucking. Is that perfect for you to grasp?"

"My God," Rachel gasped.

"Don't look so shocked, Rachel. Lem knows, and he loves it, too. Oh look, here's Morris coming."

Morris wiped his brow with a handkerchief as he strolled towards the back porch. He stopped to look back at Lem who was already working a sweat under his clothes as he continued working on his garden before letting himself through the back door into the kitchen.

Gloria was there to welcome him with open arms. Morris accepted her kiss but stopped when he saw the woman who was with him.

"Morris darling, this is Rachel. She's a good friend of mine and a neighbor."

"Pleasure," Morris shook hands with Rachel who could not keep her cheeks from glowing red.

"Likewise."

"Rachel said she was listening in on us yesterday while we fucked," Gloria chuckled as she hugged her lover. "I wonder what her thoughts would have been had she actually watched us."

"Well, now she's here, how about we give her a treat."

Gloria was all chuckles as Morris's hand delved into the opening of her dress and whipped out her breasts. Rachel was agog at the audacious move he unleashed before his eyes. She took a step back as they sauntered into the living room, kissing and fondling each other while they did. Gloria sat down on a couch and helped with undoing Morris's belt buckle. Rachel came and sat across from them to watch. Her mouth hung open with surprise when she saw her friend extract her lover's cock and into her mouth it went.

Morris winced at the impact of her lips grazing his cock.

Gloria stroked his shaft while rolling her mouth over his rod.

Rachel watched mesmerized by their activity.

Morris rested his hand on Gloria's head, guiding her to swallow more and more of his girth. He as well jerked forward his hips; he appreciated the sight of her mouth consuming his cock and the murmur of content that escaped her mouth. Gloria was too engrossed in the mood to care about the effect sucking her lover's cock was having upon Rachel. Rachel, for her part, felt a slight invasive warm feeling stealing into her body. It was a feeling she usually associated with her husband whenever they made love. But this one was acting so strange upon her, she could even feel her heart racing in her chest as she kept her eyes locked on her friend and the black man she was pleasuring.

Morris pulled back and the two of them hurried to get out of their clothes. Gloria laid back on the couch and played with her pussy. Rachel marveled at the sight of Morris's cock. She immediately feared for her friend's life as he came to his knees and lavished her pussy with his tongue and lips. Gloria moaned ecstatically as he went on pleasuring her orally. He came up for air when he was done, balanced himself then aimed his prick at her cunt. To Rachel's surprise, Gloria grabbed his cock and inserted it into her pussy for him.

"Aawhhh, aawwhhhh," Gloria moaned as Morris worked his prick into her wet box. She held onto him as he went on thrusting inside her. Her breathing hitched as he slid in deeper. "Give me that dick, babe," she breathed.

Rachel watched Morris's buttocks clench as he went ahead with fucking her friend. Her eyes were fixated between his legs at the size of his nuts and his cock enveloping Gloria's cunt that was starting to lubricate with cum. Gloria's legs locked over his thighs. Her hands smacked his buttock as she spoke to him to fuck her harder.

Morris went ahead doing just that. Gloria erupted into spasms as he rammed his girth all the way to the hilt. Her body eruption went into overdrive.

Her hips bucked against his.

She raked her fingers against his arms and shoulders.

She yelped so loud it stirred Rachel who felt herself leaking underneath her panties.

Morris got Gloria to ride him and it was his turn to smack her butt as she slammed against him harder. Gloria leaned forward, grabbed at the couch's headrest and moaned aloud as she went on rocking her pelvis back and forth on his dick

Rachel was startled when out of the corner of her eye she noticed a shadow enter the room. Once again she felt embarrassed seeing that it was Lem. He had his shirt open and was gasping from the strenuous work he had accomplished on his garden outside. He too was taken aback when he saw Rachel. He gave her a bashful smile then switched his gaze to Gloria riding her lover. Lem came and sat beside Rachel who felt somewhat uncomfortable about his presence. The sat there listening and taking awkward pleasure in watching the two people fucking in their presence.

"Hi Lem," she said to him testily.

"Nice of you to drop by, Rachel. How's Eric?"

"He's great. He went out earlier but he should be home about now," she added.

"That's good."

They sat watching Gloria whimper and holler and pelt Morris with kisses as he smacked her butt, grunting as she continued riding him. Lem and Rachel continued to sit there tense and watching as Morris began jerking his thigh and hips, fucking Gloria faster.

Minutes passed when Rachel, unable to quell the warmth she was having in her panties came to her feet. "I think I'd better be heading back home now," she spoke as if unsure of her words. "I'll tell Eric to give you a call."

"Yeah, sure," Lem stood up as well. "That will be great. Do say hello to him for me."

"I will."

Rachel turned and hurried out of the room. Her hand was jittery when she got to the front door and opened it. It felt to her like she was escaping a mad house. The screeching noise of sex seemed to follow her as she stepped into sunlight, slamming the door behind her hard. Rachel struggled to hold onto her sanity as she hurried toward home.

Eric was not there when she entered her home. She felt grateful for that; she did not want him witnessing what she had to do next. She went and locked herself in her upstairs bathroom, hiked up her skirt and proceeded to masturbate while on the toilet seat.

10

Lem received a call from his friend Eric later that evening. He had been expecting such a call all afternoon and felt relieved when it happened.

"Hi Eric. How's it going?"

"Doing great over here. Listen, can we talk? In person, I mean."

"Sure. How about we go for a drive?"

"Alright. I'll swing over right now."

"I'll be outside waiting."

They hung up after that.

Lem had minutes ago concluded eating out Gloria's pussy for the third time of the day as well cleaning Morris's cock. They were busy taking a shower when Lem changed his clothes and yelled out that he was going out. He pocketed his phone and wallet before leaving the room and marching down the stairs. The time was 06:24 p.m.

He did not have long to wait before Eric pulled over in front of his driveway in a convertible. Lem got in the passenger seat and they drove to park not far from the estate where they lived. There was fast-food joint located across the park. Eric drove there and they went inside and bought sodas and burritos. They found themselves a table away from the meagre crowd that was there. Lem waited for his friend to say something. Eric.

"You've been doing some naughty stuff, my friend."

"I take it Rachel's told you everything she saw today."

"It wasn't just what she saw, Lem," Eric looked around before describing to him what he had seen the day he was at Lem's bedroom door. "Tell me that wasn't you, Lem. Tell me you're not really... gay."

He enunciated this last word.

"I don't know, Eric. I can't say that I am… I mean I don't think of me being one in the real sense…"

"Lem, I saw you giving head to some guy," he spoke in a tight voice. "I watched you blow another man with my own fucking eyes. If I'd heard someone tell me this I'd have called bullshit. But don't tell me what I saw wasn't real."

"No, you actually did see it," Lem said. "I don't know if Rachel told you but the guy does happen to be my gardener. She saw he fuck Gloria, so I'm not denying that either, Eric."

That said, Eric felt somewhat relaxed about his friend's admission. Though the admission seemed to take away whatever steam he had in his mind he had expected to throw at his friend. It would have been a lot better if Lem had attempted some sort of denial instead of casually admitting the truth. Eric was stymied of how else to continue.

"You think I'm crazy," Lem asked. It came out as a statement but Eric misconceived it for a question.

"I'm no therapist, nor am I one to judge, Lem. Just help me understand all of this, please. Rachel was freaking out when I came home and she told me what she had witnessed in your living room."

Lem shrugged his shoulders and drank his soda. He proceeded to narrate to his friend how he had been at work one afternoon when Gloria audaciously texted him short videos of her making love to Morris in their bedroom. He had driven home in blinding rage but all of that had melted from him when Gloria told him how she and Morris had been fucking for days and only then decided to let him into the picture. Lem told Eric what he had done afterwards after she talked about wanting him to suck Morris's cock. Then had come the occasions when she hid him in their coatroom closet whenever Morris came by and he had from there spied on them fucking. Eric was all ears the whole time he talked. At one point he glanced down and saw his uneaten burrito staring at him on his plate looking neglected. He picked it up and ate half of it while soaking up his friend's tale.

Lem concluded with what had happened yesterday with Morris dropping by his home while the party went on outside and of Lem going upstairs to suck his cock after Gloria had spent some time with him.

"And that's everything," Lem said.

Eric shook his head in amazement and sighed. No way did he consider that his friend was insane or losing his marbles. He could not help but admire him to fastidiously embracing this weird part of his life like it was not strange enough; this definitely was a part of Lem he had never witnessed before. For anybody else hearing this would automatically conclude that Lem was crazy and that he Eric was just as nuts to be sitting here listening to his tale.

"I'm not shocked, but I am stunned out of my head, Lem. I don't think this soda I'm drinking will do; I'm going to need a beer just to wind down from everything you just told me."

"I don't blame you. Would you think that I won't be out of my head if someone had told me months ago that this is something I was going to be experiencing down the road?"

"I must tell you, I've seen porn videos of guys sucking other men's cocks. I don't know if they're gay or not, like you said you've done in front of Gloria and cousin."

"I haven't taken it up the ass if you really want to know," Lem laughed. That got Eric laughing too. "I know it sounds bizarre, but there's just something pleasurable taking... blowing Morris. Just tasting Gloria's juice off his cock... hell, sitting here thinking about it and saying it gets me aroused."

"You're kidding me," Eric gasped.

"You ever watched any cuckold porn before? If you haven't, then you should."

"I wasn't born yesterday, Lem. I have watched such porn before, even plenty of times. But I just don't get it. I mean, what's this crazy trend about getting aroused while some other dude is out there banging your woman? What is it really?"

"That it's not you doing the banging is what makes it worthwhile," Lem answered. "Really, you ought to consider it for Rachel," he added.

Eric wanted to say something to counter that but could not dig up the right words without sounding shrill or stupid. He clamped up instead and ate his burrito.

* * *

Rachel went and tucked her kids into bed then switched off their lights and shut their door before heading to hers. Eric was up in bed typing something on his laptop. He was dressed in his pajamas whereas Rachel was in her night dress. She came and slid into bed beside him.

"Are the kids asleep?" he asked.

"They're on their way to dreamland," she said. "What are you working on, honey?"

"A company memorandum. But don't worry, I'm almost done here."

"How was your evening with Lem?"

Eric stopped his typing and closed the lid of his laptop. "It went well; pretty interesting. Except I doubt that comes close to explaining what he told me."

Eric shared with Rachel the details of his conversation with Lem. Rachel stopped him few times for clarification before letting him continue. It did not take long for him to finish and neither said anything at first.

"Do you think he's crazy?" Rachel asked.

"No way. If he is then he's the sanest person ever to appear crazy that I know of. But I doubt he is. It's a fetish thing and somehow, Lem's caught the bug."

"Cuckold fetish?"

"Yeah. You know, men wanting their wives to screw other men while they watch. It's a growing trend out there and many people are getting involved in it."

"How do you come to know about this?"

"I've read stuff online. I mean, I've heard of people getting into it, but for the love of me, I never would have thought Lem and Gloria would be into it. I wonder how she started in it."

"Morris, the guy she's dating, is their gardener," Rachel remarked.

"He is. But if she'd doing this now, that means she's done this before without Lem being the wiser."

Eric got rid of his laptop then switched off the lights. They shared a kiss, said goodnight to each other, then fell asleep.

Rachel had told Eric everything she had witnessed with Gloria fucking her gardener. But there was plenty she had left out of her narrative. The part that concerned her masturbating when she returned home. How she had retried her dildo afterwards and worked herself to an orgasm before he arrived home from wherever he had gone and he had been none the wiser.

11

It was a Monday morning. Lem adjusted himself in his jacket. Gloria handed him his briefcase, followed by a kiss and then she walked him to the door.

"Don't forget to pick up some milk when you're coming home," she reminded him.

"I won't, darling. Don't wear him out, you hear."

He gestured with a glance of his eyes upstairs; Gloria caught the gesture with a chuckle.

"Don't worry about him. He can handle me for sure."

Lem admired his wife in her silk robe then turned and walked out of the house. Gloria watched him get into his car and waved goodbye at him as he drove off. She shut the door then returned upstairs.

Morris was in bed with the sheets draped over him. Gloria hung her robe by the door then got onto the bed. Morris did not stir even as she caressed his arm. Not to be undaunted, she pulled back the sheets, exposing his nakedness. She snaked her fingers around his penis. It felt cold and in her hand; nothing a good feeling of warmth could not handle.

Gloria changed position and drew closer to his crotch. She rolled her tongue around the tip of his penis, inhaled the exotic musky smell that wafted from his pubic hair, before then tasting his cock. Morris came awake and caressed her hair as she went on massaging his balls while feeling his member become hard in her mouth.

"Morning," Morris murmured.

working the barbeque grill and joking with several of his friends when the doorbell sounded. Lem went to open the door and was surprisingly elated to find Morris standing there.

"Good day sir," Morris said. "I'm here to work on the garden. And to enjoy your wife," he added.

"That's good of you, Morris. But I don't think tending the garden will be necessary today. Why don't you drop your bag and head on upstairs while I go over and tell Gloria you're here."

Morris did as he said while Lem hurried back the way he had come towards the kitchen. Gloria sat on a lounge chair sipping bubbly and making chatter with several of her friends who, too, were clad in bikini, frolicking by the pool. Lem said hi to the ladies then bent over Gloria and whispered briefly into her ear. Gloria raised an eye brow but maintained her cool when Lem finished his message then returned to go mend the barbeque. She remained with her friends, laughing while one of them shared an anecdote. She waited a minute before finishing her drink then decided she needed to go inside and get another bottle. Lem was conversing with a friend when he happened to turn his head and observed Gloria walking towards the back door then into the kitchen. Although he was smiling, his friend who stood beside him sharing a dirty joke never would have thought what it was that he was actually smiling about.

Gloria left her glass on a counter then raced out of the kitchen, hurried up the stairs to the main bedroom. She flung the door open and smiled when Morris turned from where he stood by the window gazing down at the party she had just left.

"I'm so happy you came," she said as she shut the door and turned the key in the lock. "This way we can be safe," she added before coming into his arms.

"You don't want your man coming in on us?"

"Nah. He's got too much to take care of downstairs," she said as she wrapped her arms around his neck and kissed him. "It's time you got to take care of me. But we'll have to hurry." She reached behind her back to unclasp her bra. "I don't want any of my friends to start wondering why I'm taking so long to return."

* * *

"Morning, babe," said Gloria. She turned over to face him while still cradling his cock. "I needed me some morning snack. I hope you don't mind."

No way was Morris going to say no to that. Gloria continued with enjoying every inch of his throbbing cock, loving the smell of it, loving the way it kicked against her chin as it grew further turgid.

She dove a hand between her legs to rub her pussy.

She moaned as she felt herself become wet.

She could not wait to get his cock inside her.

Gloria slid forward on top of him. Morris held her by her waist; his cock found its own way inside her pussy. Gloria flung her head backward, loving the exquisite feel of his prick slipping inside her womb. She worked her hips up and down and side to side as he went deep brushing against her cervix.

"Aww… you're so big, darling. Uuhhh… Uhhhh… so fucking good."

Gloria gasped and continued mouthing off her train of thought as Morris started jerking his hips, pounding her pussy hard. He squeezed her tits in both hands. She caressed his arms and torso. She loved the feel of his shoulder muscles—so strong, so black and beautiful—so unlike her husband's flabby which she so despised. Gloria fell into Morris's arms; she could remain here all day with his cock jammed inside her and she would not miss a thing.

Their tempo increased. Their fucking became rough and energetic. Gloria loved it. Morris turned her over and they wrestled each other for dominance. Morris grabbed her wrists and pinned her down, overpowered her, and fucked her harder. Gloria hooked her legs over his backside.

"More," she gasped, jerking her hips in sync with his movement. "Give it to me, darling."

Morris grunted against her face.

He breathed upon her lips.

Her lips opened and accepted his kiss.

He slipped his hands underneath her buttocks and propped her lower body against his. Morris fucked her as hard as his thigh muscles could muster. Gloria felt his cock expand in her pussy and knew he was about to cum. Morris pulled out and came forward and jerked his cock frantically against her face. Gloria already had her mouth open. His first salvo landed on her tongue. Morris groaned as he went on jerking his meat, pumping spurt after spurt of semen down her throat. Gloria swallowed every drop.

DINNGGG-DOOONNNGGGG!

The sound of the doorbell signaled an end to their morning tryst.

"Who the devil could that be now," Gloria huffed.

"Probably your husband forgot something?" asked Morris.

"He usually doesn't, but it won't be the first time. Don't go nowhere, darling."

Gloria kissed Morris then got up from bed. She wore back her robe and left the room. The doorbell sounded off again as she went down the stairs. She peeped through the window before opening the door.

"Rachel," she said.

,

12

Rachel saw her kids off to school. She waited until Eric was out of the house and off to work before setting about her mission. This was twenty minutes before Lem came out of his front door. She went and grabbed her husband's laptop and carried it with her to the living room.

One thing Eric probably never would have figured was how quick Rachel had grasped the slip of tongue he had made last night in bed. Rachel had laid in bed last night spooning his words in the back of her head and somewhere between being awake and slipping into deep sleep she had sworn to get to the bottom of his words without him knowing. Eric definitely would be nervous had he any idea what she intended doing this morning.

Rachel was not completely dumb with regards to what her husband did with his relaxing time. She was well aware of how much he loved watching porn. So many times he had tried to get her hooked onto watching along with him. Rachel recalled times when they had gotten drunk and watched one or two clips before retiring to bed to make love. No way would Eric have given up that habit now, she was quite sure of that. Especially from what he had mentioned last night which added toward getting her mind percolating to finding out herself.

She opened the laptop's lid and went searching into his video folder. There were typical videos there, most having to deal with his work and others of family. Rachel stumbled upon three password-enclosed folders there. It took her few attempts to figure out the simple password to unlock them. She was not disappointed by what she found in them.

There were videos.

Porn videos.

Hundreds of them.

Rachel gasped as she scrolled through each folder, marveling at how many there were. It would probably take her a month to look through everything in her husband's collection. Some were short videos while others were porn flicks he had downloaded from wherever, all bearing distinct names: SUCK MY TWAT Vol. 3… SHE LOVES IT BLACK… ANAL ADVENTURES #23… HOTWIVES LOVE BLACK COCKS… MASTER SHANGO'S SLAVE PETS #3…

Rachel felt dizzy reading out the names. She clicked on several and watched them play out. Majority of the videos were of interracial variety: featuring black men making love to white women of different age. She recognized several showcasing the cuckold fetish Eric had mentioned yesterday: husbands offering their wives to have sex with black men. Rachel was not stupid. She had never once invested a serious thought into the artificiality inherent in porn flicks… but after what she had witnessed with Lem and Gloria and her lover, it made her reconsider just how serious people considered this trend. That possibility included Eric. Why else would have such a large stash of interracial/cuckold movies?

She recalled the strange, illicit sensation she felt yesterday while watching Gloria fuck her lover. The image had stayed on her mind when she raced back home to masturbate. How wonderful that moment felt. She tried to imagine whatever audacity might have inspired Gloria into doing that in the first place without fear of any consequences.

Rachel watched another video. This one showed a muscular black man fucking a white blonde in bed while her husband knelt by the foot of the bed watching them. The black man climaxed inside the blonde and then made room for the husband who then got on the bed and lapped his tongue on the woman's pussy.

Disgusting!

But suddenly she could not stop herself from being moved by it. Even now she felt it drumming in her body again, like a magnetic wave stirring inside her panties. Rachel's hand stole into her shorts to touch herself. It felt so good the feel of her wet flesh. How long was it been since she and Eric fooled around? With the kids, such moments were usually far and few in-between. How would he respond if like Lem he got to find out she had decided to become like one of the many women in his porn stash?

There was only one way to find out.

Rachel closed the laptop's lid then left the house.

She had no way of knowing if Gloria might be home or not. It was her mistake—she should have called first. She pressed the doorbell then waited. Minutes later she pressed it a second time. The door opened and Gloria revealed herself.

"Rachel," Gloria said.

13

"I need to talk to you, Gloria," Rachel said. "It's important."

Gloria ushered her friend into her home then shut the door. "Go wait in the living room. I need to make breakfast for Morris."

"Is he here already?" Rachel asked with a surprised look that Gloria found too hilarious not to laugh at.

"Of course he's here. He spent the night; he's free to come whenever he wants. Just wait for me, I'll get you some coffee when I'm done."

Rachel went to go sit in the living room while Gloria headed toward the kitchen. Inside, she brewed a pot a coffee, fried some bacon and eggs then made some toast. She poured a glass of fruit juice and when she was done carried the plate on a tray up the stairs to her bedroom. Morris was out of the bathroom drying himself with a towel when she walked in.

"I brought you something to eat." She laid the tray on a coffee table and brought it close to the bed. "Do you have to leave so soon?"

"Not too soon." He discarded the towel them came and sat by the bed in front of the breakfast meal. "I have to be at my other job by noon though."

"What's this other job you're working?"

"I drive a home delivery truck. Boring stuff."

"Have you begun using that credit card I gave you last time?"

"A little. Were you being serious about it?"

"Of course I was. Why do you think I gave it to you? I'll have Lem wire you some money when he returns home."

Morris forked some bacon into his mouth then took a sip of the fruit drink. "You know you really shouldn't."

"I shouldn't, true. But I want to. Anyway, let's talk about it later. Go ahead and eat your breakfast. My friend Rachel is downstairs waiting for me."

She left the room and returned to the kitchen and made herself two cups of coffee and took them to the living room.

"I added cream and honey to both," she said as she handed Rachel her cup. "I hope you don't mind."

"No, I don't. Thanks."

They stirred their coffee and took sips from their cup.

"Hmm, tastes good," Rachel said. "Lem didn't quarrel with you about having Morris around?"

"Are you kidding? Lem wants nothing more than to keep seeing us in bed together," Gloria laughed. "But enough of that. You said there was something important you wanted to talk to me about. What is it?"

Rachel looked away for a moment. "It's complicated, I thought I knew just how to begin but now... I'm kinda at a loss."

"Does any of it have to do with yesterday?" Gloria inquired.

"Yeah, kind of. But I think it's got more to do with just that. Yesterday is probably what opened the thought for me. After I watched you guys fuck, I ran back home and... and I sat in the toilet and masturbated." Rachel blushed with embarrassment when she uttered this last part. "I know I shouldn't say that, but I think you're the right person to tell," she quickly added.

"Awwh, Rachel. Why didn't you say that in the first place? Listen, I get how you say you felt then. The same could have happened to me if I'd been you, and there's nothing to be ashamed about."

"That's part of the problem I'm having. I don't know exactly what to feel about it, or really if I should. Last night, Eric and I talked about this whole thing. This morning I looked in his computer and saw he's got thousands of videos on this cuckold stuff. You know, husbands watching as other men—mostly black men—screw their eyes in front of them. Either that or it's interracial couples fucking."

Neither woman said anything at first. Eventually Gloria broached the question. "You're thinking Eric has had this idea on his mind for you?"

"I reckon so. I know he once used to get me to watch some of his porn with him, and for a while I did. But I got turned off afterwards. I don't remember if he's ever mentioned this before, but I'd be dumb to think he hasn't thought about it. They were all I saw in his computer."

"That's surprising."

"Was it ever like this for you and Lem when you first started..."

"You mean with Morris? I had dared him on it a couple of times before, but he never thought I'd take it serious. He kinda dared me to do it, which I did. When I sent him a video of us fucking, he knew then just how serious I was about this."

"And he's never gotten upset since?"

"Not as long as I've known him. You can say it was all meant to happen that he'd somehow get to love it."

"Do you think Eric might feel the same way if he found out that I've done such?"

Gloria caught the beseeching plea in her friend's eyes and wondered if really she was ready to cross that line.

"Only one way to find out," Gloria said. "But that's only if you're willing. Come with me."

She took her friend's hand and together they left the room and went upstairs.

14

Morris finished tying his shoes laces then got up and wore his shirt. He looked around the room for his garden tools bag, found it, and then slung it over his shoulder. He was almost at the door when it opened and there stood Gloria with her friend Rachel shuffling beside her. Rachel's cheeks were flush red when she laid eyes on Morris. She still could not fathom how Gloria was capable of having such a handsome young man all to herself without any repercussion to her marriage. None whatsoever.

"Hey there," Gloria pressed a hand against her lover's chest, pushing him backward. "Where do you think you're going, hot shot?"

"It's getting late already," Morris said. "I told you already I've got to be at my next job by noon."

"Aw, you really want to go and leave me all here alone with myself? And I've even brought my friend over to spend time with. You remember Rachel, don't you? Rachel, say hello to my darling Morris."

They said hello to each other and shook hands. Rachel's cheeks felt like nuclear reactors about to explode. She turned her face away from Morris. Making eye contact with him seemed to ignite the weird sensations stirring in her loins, making it more fervent than last time. Her nerves were on fire and her palms were turning sweaty. She would have turned and left the room were Gloria not holding her arm.

"Rachel here has got a sudden urge to take some black meat," Gloria continued. "I know you're in a hurry, darling, but would you do me this small favor of making her feel special?"

"You're kidding, right?"

"No, I'm not. Please do this for me. I promise to make it worth your while later."

Morris looked at her, then his eyes went to Rachel still attempting her best to avoid eye contact with him.

"She doesn't look like she wants it," Morris said.

"Oh yes, she does," Gloria answered. "She only needs a little bit of warming up."

Gloria undid the sash of her robe and let it fall to the floor. She then turned to Rachel. "How about we get you out of these," she indicated at her top.

Rachel looked at her friend with maddening eyes like she could not believe her opening up to Gloria had now led to this. She would have loved to protest but her body betrayed her by failing to respond. Even worst was when Morris came and stood beside her. Like Gloria, he, too, had his hands pulling at her tank top. Rachel raised both arms, allowing them to peel it off her head.

"There, that's good," Gloria murmured. "Next we've got to loosen that bra you're wearing."

Rachel felt the hairs on the back of her neck stand erect as Morris's breath fell on her shoulder. He too assisted Gloria with getting rid of her bra, the whole time Rachel said nothing as she soon stood half naked in their presence.

"Let's take her to bed, darling," Gloria suggested.

Morris dropped his tools bag and with that started getting out of his clothes. Gloria sat her friend on the bed and helped her out of the rest of her clothes. Rachel muttered under her breath but still gave no fight as she slipped out of her panties. She looked over at Morris and gasped at the sight of his cock as he shoved his briefs along with his jeans down his thighs.

Gloria was already fondling her breasts, getting her further excited. Rachel's hand went to her pussy and it came back with dripping wetness.

"It'll be best if you lie down," said Gloria soothingly. "Try to relax."

Rachel did lie on her back but she was far from being relax. Even with Gloria kissing her tits and now rubbing her clit, she felt like a mix-bag of tension and arousal. Her concentration remained focused on Morris who was busy pulling his feet out of his shoes. His cock appeared semi-erect, hanging aslant of his crotch. Rachel already was projecting in her mind the assault she was about to receive. Her eyes followed Morris as he came and sat beside her. Like Gloria, he too spent some time sucking on her other pair of breasts. Rachel flung her head backward and moaned. Her body spasmed and tensed as their lips pulled on her nipples. Morris too probed her pussy with his fingers. He slid downward on the bed and propped her feet over his shoulder and proceeded to further stimulate her pussy with his tongue. Rachel's moaning frenzy went into overdrive. Her body jerked in line with Morris flickering the tip of his tongue against the rip bud that was her clitoris. Gloria pressed her body against hers, murmuring at her not to fret too much.

"Don't worry, Rachel. It'll all be over soon… you're doing great… do you like it? Yes, I know you do."

Rachel was immediately drowning in a rampaging sea of ecstasy though she was grateful for Gloria's sweet-talking voice as it was the only thing her mind could grasp at that prevented her from completely losing herself even though that seemed hard with the effortless manner Morris worked on her pussy. She could not control the spasms as they racked her womb. It felt to her like she was being stabbed by a thousand daggers. She wanted to scream badly; she wanted to swim against the tide…

Gloria came down from the bed to join Morris and together they took turns pleasuring Rachel. Morris slid forward on the bed and held up Rachel's head and stuck his cock into her mouth. Rachel offered no resistance to this. Her lips made contact with the tip of his penis then parted ways for it to slip inside the cavern that was her mouth and waiting tongue. It would have surprised her then were she still in full control of herself that aside from her husband Eric, Rachel had only given blowjobs twice in her life. She was inexperienced in the act and her only feeble effort was to roll her tongue over Morris's foreskin as he went ahead with thrusting his shaft in and out of her mouth.

Morris grabbed her feet and pulled her towards him. He didn't want to waste any time fucking her. Rachel barely had time to tense against him when his prick sought her pussy and then drove home inside her.

"Aaawwhhhh!"

Rachel screamed the instant she felt his cock begin to stretch her pussy muscles. At one point she thought he had stopped and her body relaxed somewhat. But it was only for Morris to adjust himself between her spread legs before then pressing ahead. He tore further into her pussy. Tight as it was, it resisted momentarily, though soon he broke through. Rachel whimpered and gasped harder as she felt his cock reaching towards her cervix. It was going places no penis before had ever been, not even her husband. Her eyes rolled in their sockets and she slammed her head on the bed.

"Awwhhh... Oh my God! Ooohhhhh my fucking God!"

Rachel gasped aloud as Morris grunted on top of her. Gloria was there beside her, caressing her face as she went on taking the brute shaft piercing her cunt back and forth. Rachel felt her womb set ablaze. The stirring she had earlier felt was at octane level; she climaxed in record time.

15

"So what happened?" Lem asked.

"I told you just about everything already," Gloria replied. "What do you think happened?"

"I don't know. I wasn't here to watch, remember. I figured maybe afterwards he got to fuck her some more."

"That he did," Gloria chuckled. "That was before she left."

The time was 10:15 p.m. Lem knew he ought to be asleep already but Gloria had kept him up with salacious details of the romp she had enjoyed with Rachel and Morris. Especially the part of Morris fucking her in their bed while Gloria soothed Rachel to keep taking his dick. Lem had been lost for words when Gloria called him up during lunch hour to mention it to him. She did keep mum regarding the details until he returned home, and only an hour ago when they had settled in bed.

"My God, she actually took every inch of his cock?"

"I won't say she took everything," Gloria teased. She was caressing his cock under the sheets, jerking him while she spoke. "She isn't a pro like me, but she did take enough of him. He made her cum twice."

"You're shitting me," Lem gasped.

"Uh-uh. He did make her cum twice; she even said it. You should have seen her when she left here," Gloria crackled.

"What do you mean?"

"She was practically walking with a limp when she left," Gloria laughed aloud. "I think she'll be back again."

"Awwwh, I wish I was here to see it happen."

Gloria jerked him to climax after which he went to the bathroom to clean himself off then returned to bed, switching off the lights while he did.

The End